This Book Belongs To

1 fact

Christmas is an annual Christian holiday that honors the birth of Jesus Christ. The Roman Catholic Church chose December 25 as His birthday many years after His death. This Christian holiday is celebrated by Christians around the world

How interesting is this?

Color the matching face

2 fact

Christmas trees were first used by the ancient Egyptians and Romans. They used evergreen trees such as fir or pine, wreaths and garlands. Modern Christmas trees began to be used in Germany in the 16th century. Instead of the shiny ornaments we see on them today, they were decorated with fruits and nuts

How interesting is this?

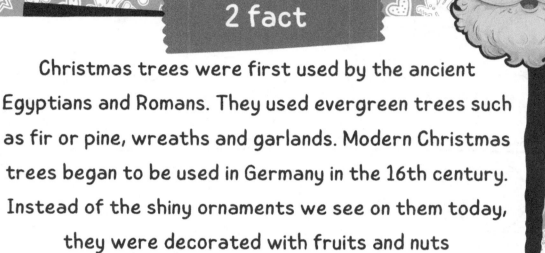

Color the matching face

3 fact

Santa Claus did not always dress in red clothes. Santa Claus originally wore green, purple or blue clothes. Some claim that the modern image of Santa Claus was created by Coca-Cola, but this is not strictly true. The original red Santa became popular in the US and Canada in the 19th century

How interesting is this?

Color the matching face

4 fact

When Jesus was born, a bright star shone in the sky. The three kings followed this star and made the long journey to the place where Jesus was born. They brought with them gifts of gold, frankincense and myrrh.

How interesting is this?

Color the matching face

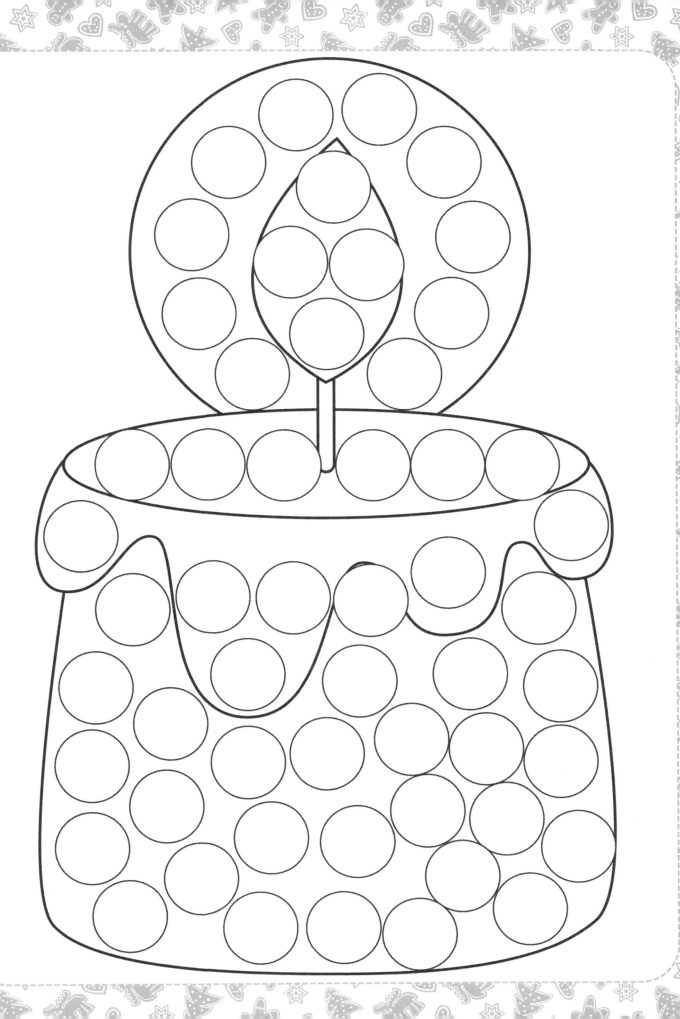

5 fact

Santa Claus comes with gifts for children who have been good all year. But did you know that Santa Claus also gets gifts? Who gives gifts to Santa Claus? Us! Yes, even you can give gifts to Santa! And no, this jolly old man doesn't want traditional gifts, but he likes cookies and milk to keep him happy as he travels around the world.

How interesting is this?

Color the matching face

6 fact

One of the reasons Santa can run his marathon in a day and distribute gifts to children around the world is the help of elves. The merry spirit of Christmas is due to these cheerful employees and their commitment to children around the world.

How interesting is this?

Color the matching face

7 fact

The most popular carol is "Silent Night," which is known all over the world. It is translated in more than 300 languages.

How interesting is this?

Color the matching face

8 fact

The traditional colors of Christmas are three: green, red and gold. The first symbolizes life and rebirth. The red color refers to the blood of Jesus Christ, while gold is a symbol of light and prosperity

How interesting is this?

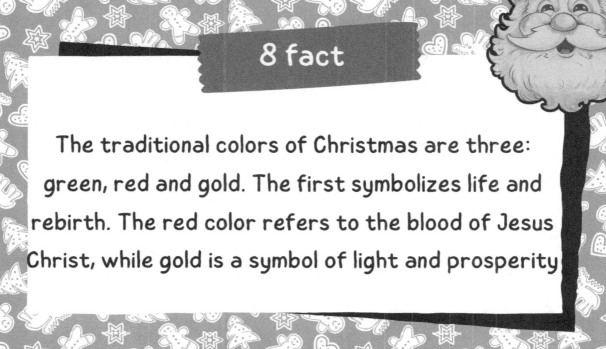

Color the matching face

9 fact

In every home gifts are piled under the Christmas tree, and they are opened on Christmas morning before breakfast. The climax of Christmas is a festive dinner, at which the closer and further family must not be absent.

How interesting is this?

Color the matching face

10 fact

The tradition is to hang mistletoe from the ceiling and kiss under it. It is said that kissing under the mistletoe brings good luck for the next year.

How interesting is this?

Color the matching face

11 fact

In the Catholic Church at midnight there is a midnight shepherdess, which marks the birth of Jesus. Advent ends and a time of great joy for the birth of Jesus begins. It is characterized by lights in the church being turned off, which are gradually turned on while carols are sung.

How interesting is this?

Color the matching face

The largest Christmas tree in the world is located in Dortmund (Germany) and is built every each year for the Christmas market.

How interesting is this?

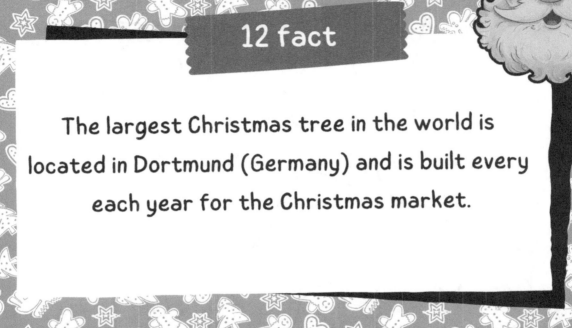

Color the matching face

13 fact

The real Santa Claus was a bishop, but his figure did not appear in pop culture until 1823 in Clement Moore's poem "A Visit from Santa Claus."

How interesting is this?

Color the matching face

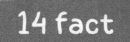

14 fact

Santa's most popular reindeer, Rudolph, was born in 1939. It was then that Robert L. May wrote a book about the adventures of this red-nosed animal. The book was immensely popular and as many as 6 million copies were printed and distributed in the first few years after its publication.

How interesting is this?

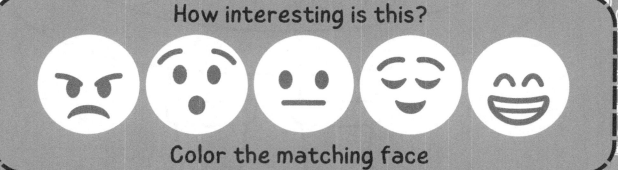

Color the matching face

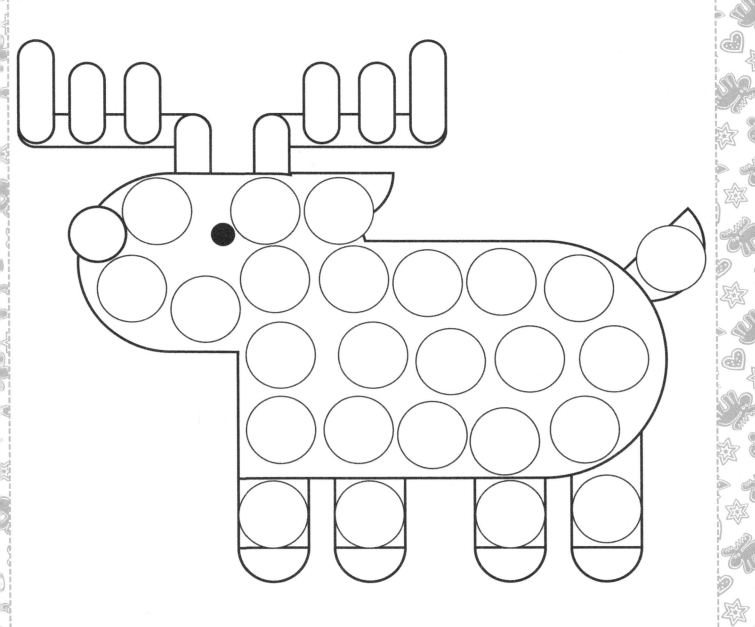

The first Christmas card was created in 1843. Its author was the British illustrator John Callcott Horsley. It gave rise to an entire tradition of sending Christmas wishes.

How interesting is this?

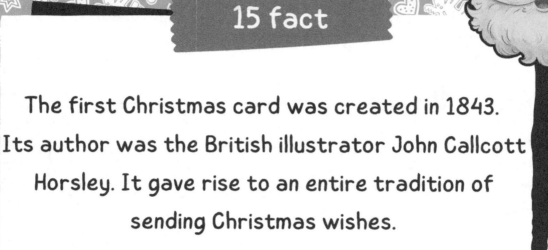

Color the matching face

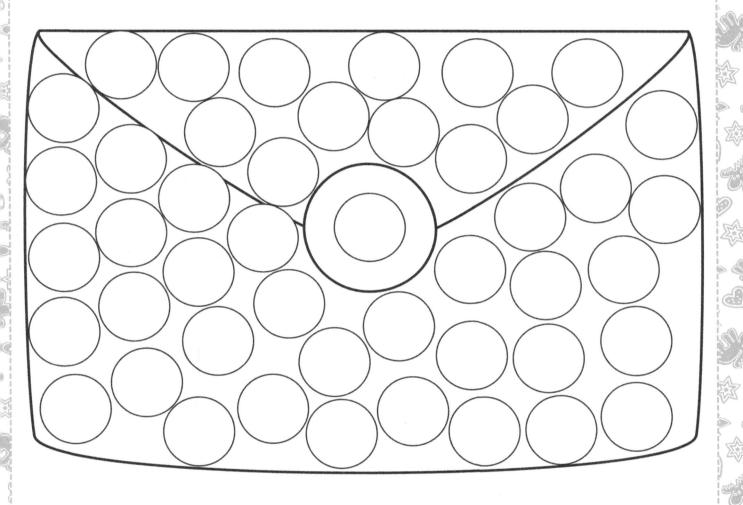

16 fact

America's official national Christmas tree is located in King's Canyon National Park in California. The Christmas tree, is more than 90 meters high.

How interesting is this?

Color the matching face

17 fact

The world's largest gift sock measured 32.56 meters long and was 14.97 meters wide. It weighed as much as five adult reindeer and held nearly 1,000 gifts. It was made by children in London on December 14, 2007.

How interesting is this?

Color the matching face

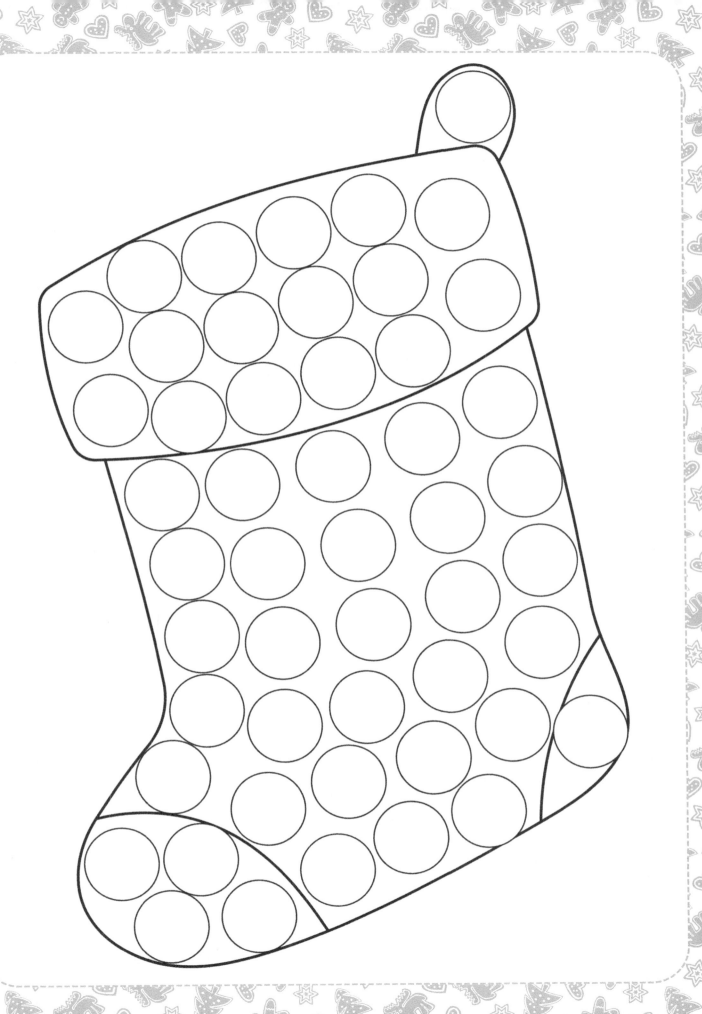

Japan has a tradition of eating on Christmas Eve of the world's popular... KFC

How interesting is this?

Color the matching face

19 fact

An interesting part of the Christmas tradition in England is the Christmas Cracker, which is a cardboard roll wrapped in colored paper, resembling candy, which makes a distinctive crackling sound when opened. Small gifts are placed in it.

How interesting is this?

Color the matching face

The period leading up to Christmas is called Advent.
It is three weeks long (four Sundays to be exact).
In Christian churches, it is a time of waiting for the
second coming of Christ.

How interesting is this?

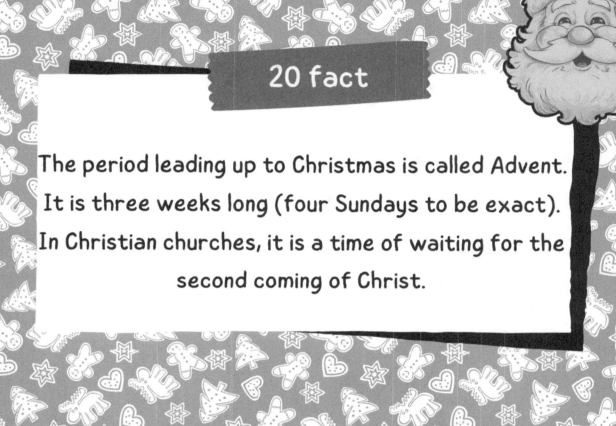

Color the matching face

21 fact

A few weeks before this holiday, nativity scenes are built in every major and minor city. The first known nativity scene was created in 1224 by Saint Francis of Assisi. Using it, Francis wanted to explain to the faithful what the miracle of Christmas was all about.

How interesting is this?

Color the matching face

Bolivians participate in the Misa del Gallo, or "Mass of the Rooster." Some people bring roosters to the shepherdess service - a gesture that symbolizes the belief that the rooster was the first animal to announce the birth of Jesus.

How interesting is this?

Color the matching face

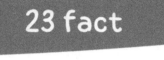

23 fact

Christmas traditions are not the same everywhere. People in Australia and New Zealand, due to their geographic location, often spend the holidays barbecuing on beaches. Spaniards, on the other hand, hold the world's oldest lottery.

How interesting is this?

Color the matching face

24 fact

One of the most popular Christmas decorations in the world are red and white candies in the shape of a shepherd's staff. The first candies of this type were produced in the 17th century in Cologne, Germany, to be distributed to children during church ceremonies.

How interesting is this?

Color the matching face

Bonus fact

We hope these Christmas facts have reminded you why Christmas is the most wonderful time of the year. Christmas facts are just an addition to the extra ounce of kindness that people are more likely to show during the holidays. However, it would be better if we had this aura and attitude all year round.

How interesting is this?

Color the matching face

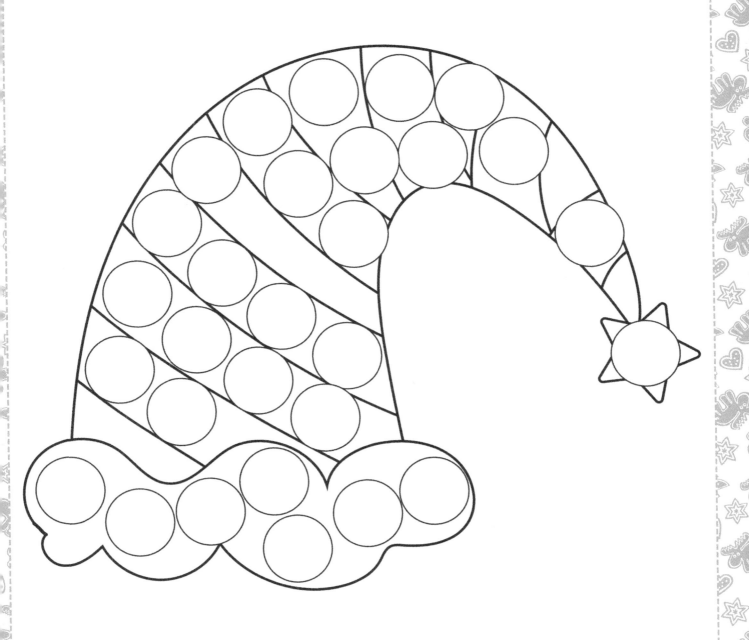

Find the words

A	M	T	W	K	U	O	I	Z	O	D	F	X	W	T	A
N	Y	P	S	D	M	W	E	W	Y	M	R	C	N	W	K
Z	C	M	Q	B	G	T	L	D	I	T	E	H	Y	F	M
C	W	A	L	W	A	S	Q	A	U	K	E	E	T	L	V
J	H	Y	I	R	I	M	Y	R	R	H	Z	S	F	S	T
T	A	Y	O	G	S	P	I	R	I	T	I	T	L	A	I
A	S	C	B	L	E	S	S	I	N	G	N	N	E	B	Z
P	E	L	P	K	F	X	R	Z	R	Z	G	U	S	M	B
D	Z	P	W	U	U	B	D	X	N	V	J	T	E	N	Q
G	P	P	E	A	C	E	D	O	V	E	N	S	A	K	R
D	M	Z	G	B	F	H	G	I	V	I	N	G	S	D	M
F	R	A	S	J	E	R	U	S	A	L	E	M	O	I	I
V	B	I	R	T	H	I	P	Q	O	B	N	D	N	J	U
T	H	O	L	I	D	A	Y	G	A	L	A	T	A	V	J
V	C	W	V	S	Y	M	B	O	L	I	Z	E	L	B	I
J	X	A	R	E	I	N	D	E	E	R	P	U	M	O	Y

BIRTH	BLESSING
CHESTNUTS	DECORATE
EAT	FREEZING
GIVING	HOLIDAY GALA
JERUSALEM	MYRRH
PEACE DOVE	REINDEER
SEASONAL	SPIRIT
SYMBOLIZE	

Find the way

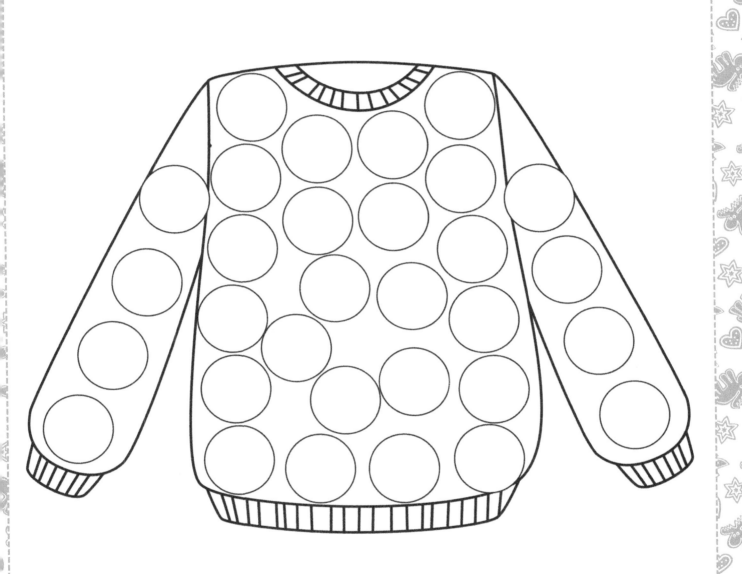

Crossword puzzle

Across

3. Festive Headwear

4. Small Gift-Makers

5. December Job

Down

1. Toy Workshop Supervisor

2. Santa's Helpers

Word Bank

Elves ElfHat HeadElf ElfWork MiniElve

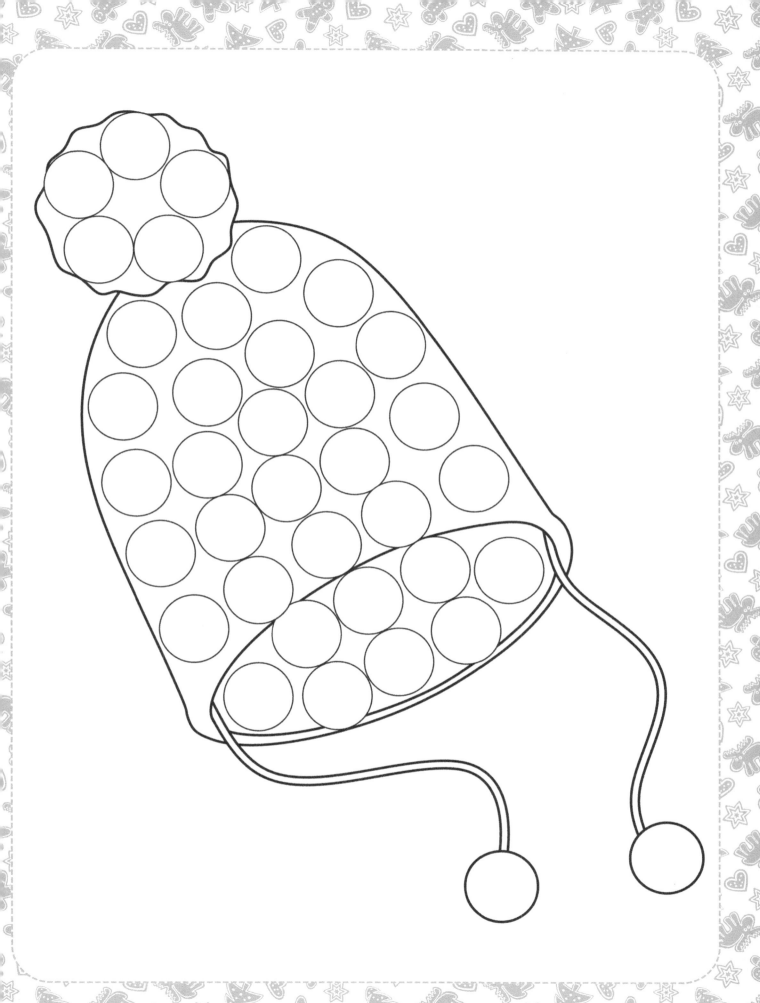

Made in the USA
Las Vegas, NV
29 November 2023

81814495R00033